Gabe
Gets His
Cape

EMY PAVELKA JONES
Illustrated by Ayin Visitacion

To order additional copies of this book, contact:
Xlibris
844-714-8691
www.Xlibris.com
Orders@Xlibris.com

ISBN: Softcover   978-1-6641-2386-1
         Hardcover   978-1-6641-2387-8
         EBook   978-1-6641-2385-4

Print information available on the last page

Rev. date: 08/11/2020

Once upon a time, and far, far away,

Where the waves of the oceans would jump and play,

There lived a little superhero named Gabriel Lee,

With the heart of a warrior and eyes like the sea.

His superhero parents could not wait to see

What little Gabe's superpowers would possibly be.

But for now that wasn't their top concern.

They just wanted to love him and help him to learn.

4

However, little Gabe had one thing on his mind.

Something was missing, something he just had to find.

His parents had something that he did not,

A treasure that he wanted a whole, whole lot.

You see, Mom and Dad had a cape so grand.

Little Gabe wanted one too, so he plotted and planned.

His parents assured him it would happen one day,

If only that one day could be today!

Gabe tried to be patient, but he just couldn't wait.

Could this superhero thing happen at a faster rate?

He would say as he gazed at their capes up so high

"I'll never get one if I don't even try".

"Dad and Mom, tell me the secret to being like you.

I want to do all of the things that you do.

I know I can do them, and I'm sure you'll agree,

Look at my superpowers! Watch me and see!"

So Gabe set off to show them the things he could do.

I'm sure if you saw him, you'd be impressed too!

"Look, Dad! Gabe said, "Look up! Watch me fly!

Surely I'll get my cape if I fly THIS high!"

"Wow, Son! That IS really great!

But I'm afraid that you still may have some time to wait."

"Mom, I can lift your car! Don't I look strong?

Will I get my cape soon? I hope it won't be too long!"

"My, that is really something, son,

But your cape will show up when the right time comes."

"Dad, what if I run as fast as can be? What if I swim across the big, blue sea?"

"Gabe, my son, come sit with me.

You've been working so hard, it's easy to see.

These deeds are outstanding, and I'm super impressed,

But being a superhero isn't like taking a test.

Becoming a real hero is SO much more.

It's more than just winning or getting a high score."

"Being a superhero is not easy to do,

But anyone can do it, yes, even you.

If you really, really want to know where to start,

Remember your powers must come from the heart."

20

Gabe was so sad and he wanted to quit!

But he did not let himself throw a big fit.

"This superhero thing is so hard to do!

Now poor little Gabe was feeling blue.

22

Mom told her sad little son, "Just go have some fun!"

So Gabe read a book, and relaxed in the sun.

He went for a walk before it got dark,

And picked up some trash that he found in the park.

When a neighbor's puppy started running away,

Little Gabe brought it back and saved the day.

28

One day when he saw a child with no smile,

Gabe talked to her and made her laugh for awhile.

As his parents said "Good Night" and put him to bed,

He gave them a hug and kissed their sweet heads.

The next morning when he woke and the sun shone bright,

Little Gabe saw the most incredible sight!

"Look, Dad and Mom! I'm just like you!

I got my cape! Now I have so much to do!"

"Yes, you did, son! We're so proud of you!

It looks like you're ready to change the world, too.

Thinking of others was a GREAT way to start.

You've found your superpowers in your heart."

So that's Gabe's story, now how about you?

Would you like to be a superhero, too?

Well, if you really, really want to know where to start,

Remember your powers must come from the heart.

GABE'S GUIDE TO SUPERPOWERS

Love

Have Fun

Read

Learn

Be kind

Give a hug

Help

Do Your Best

Make someone smile!

"A superhero's powers come from the heart"

A
SUPERHERO'S
POWERS COME
FROM THE
HEART

The End

Lightning Source UK Ltd.
Milton Keynes UK
UKHW051532020920
368892UK00015B/5